For our Little Mate
~ C.W.

LITTLE TIGER PRESS
1 The Coda Centre, 189 Munster Road, London SW6 6AW
www.littletiger.co.uk

First published in Great Britain in 1997
This edition published 2007

Text and illustrations copyright © Catherine Walters 1997
Catherine Walters has asserted her right to be identified
as the author and illustrator of this work under
the Copyright, Designs and Patents Act, 1988

A CIP catalogue record for this book is available from
the British Library

Printed in China • LTP/1800/1556/0716

2 4 6 8 10 9 7 5 3 1

When will it be Spring?

CATHERINE WALTERS

LITTLE TIGER PRESS
London

"Come inside, Alfie," said Mother Bear. "It's time
to sleep and when you wake up it will be Spring."
"When will it be Spring?" asked Alfie, "and how
will I know when it's here?"
And Mother Bear replied, "When the flowers come
out and the bees and the butterflies are hovering
overhead, then it will be Spring."

So Alfie snuggled down
to sleep . . .

but when he woke up
Alfie could not tell if Spring had
come or not. He tiptoed across the floor
of the cave, rubbed his bleary
eyes and saw . . .

. . . BUTTERFLIES!

"It's Spring! It's Spring!" cried Alfie.
"Wake up, Mother Bear!
Look at all the butterflies
and flowers!"

But when Mother Bear came out she
could only see the soft fall of new snow.
"Winter has hardly begun," she said.
"Go back to sleep, Alfie."
"But when *will* it be Spring?" Alfie
wanted to know.
And Mother Bear mumbled sleepily,
"When the swallows arrive and the birds
begin to sing, *then* it will be Spring."

Then Alfie curled up
again to sleep . . .

and when he woke
he was sure it must be
time for Spring.

He crept across the floor,
peered outside
and saw . . .

. . . BIRDS IN THE TREES!

"Mother Bear, wake up!" squealed Alfie.
"Spring is here! The birds are singing in
the trees."

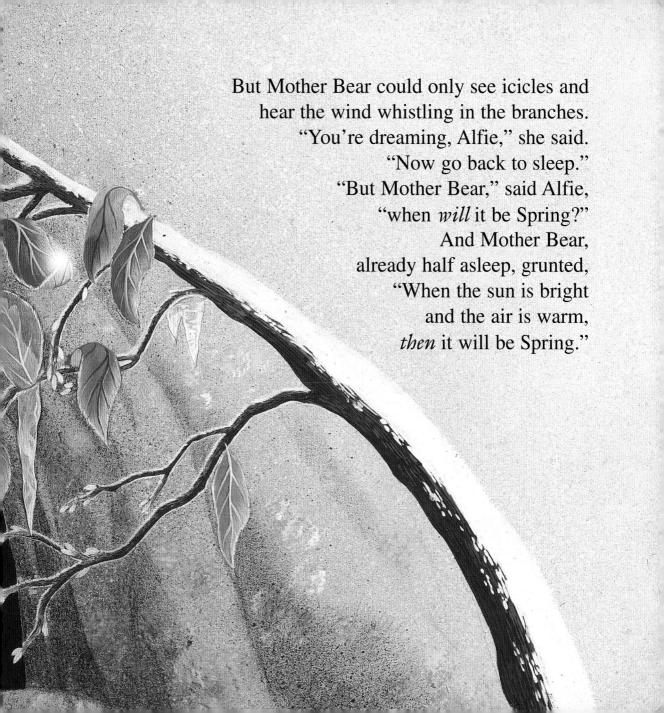

But Mother Bear could only see icicles and
hear the wind whistling in the branches.
"You're dreaming, Alfie," she said.
"Now go back to sleep."
"But Mother Bear," said Alfie,
"when *will* it be Spring?"
And Mother Bear,
already half asleep, grunted,
"When the sun is bright
and the air is warm,
then it will be Spring."

So Alfie burrowed down in his bed again . . .

and when he woke he was quite sure
Spring was here. He padded across the floor,
looked out and saw . . .

. . . A BRIGHT SUN!

"Mother Bear, you've overslept!"
cried Alfie. "Wake up! Spring is here,
the sun's out and it's beautifully warm!"

But Mother Bear could only
see the hunters' fires and
quickly hustled him away.
"Now go to sleep!" she said.
"I will tell you when
Spring is here."

So Alfie slept and dreamed of butterflies, birds and
sunshine till something icy touched his nose!
A tiny stream of water was trickling
through the cave.
Alfie shook his mother awake and she growled,
"For the very last time, Alfie, it is *not* Spring."

But Alfie patted her
hopefully until she got up,
stomped through
the doorway,

and saw . . .

. . . THE SPRING!

Mother Bear rubbed her eyes and
blinked in the warm bright light.
"Spring is here after all," she smiled.
"But *where* is Alfie?"